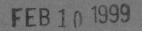

09-BTN-557

Daphne Eloise Slater, Who's Tall for Her Age

by **Gina Willner-Pardo**
Illustrated by **Glo Coalson**

Clarion Books/New York

Clarion Books
a Houghton Mifflin Company imprint
215 Park Avenue South, New York, NY 10003
Text copyright © 1997 by Gina Willner-Pardo
Illustrations copyright © 1997 by Glo Coalson

The illustrations for this book were executed in watercolor with colored pencils.
The text is set in 14.5/19-point Horley.

For information about this and other Houghton Mifflin trade and reference books
and multimedia products, visit The Bookstore at Houghton Mifflin
on the World Wide Web at (http://www.hmco.com/trade/).

Printed in the USA

Library of Congress Cataloging-in-Publication Data

Willner-Pardo, Gina.
    Daphne Eloise Slater, who's tall for her age / by Gina Willner-Pardo ;
illustrated by Glo Coalson.
        p.   cm.
    Summary: Daphne didn't mind being the tallest girl in her class
until third grade, when a classmate begins teasing her about her height
and she must decide whether to retaliate.
    ISBN 0-395-73080-5
    [1. Size—Fiction. 2. Behavior—Fiction. 3. Schools—Fiction.]
I. Coalson, Glo, ill.   II. Title.
PZ7.W6856DAp   1996
[Fic]—dc20
                                                            95-44050
                                                            CIP
                                                            AC

WOZ   10 9 8 7 6 5 4 3 2 1

For Karen Noel and her 1993–1994 second graders,
who didn't get any eyeball on me.
—G.W-P.

To Gay Mallon, for her compassion and for her wisdom.
—G.C.

Chapter 1

Daphne Eloise Slater loved everything about third grade except for Leonard DiMaggio. He was the rottenest kid in third grade.

It started the first day of school.

"Daphne Slater," Mrs. Jefferson called, looking up from her list.

Daphne was just about to raise her hand when Leonard DiMaggio pointed at her.

"That one," he said. "The one that looks like a giraffe."

"Quiet, class," Mrs. Jefferson said to get everyone to quit laughing.

Daphne had never been laughed at before, except in second grade, when she'd told Mrs. DeForrest how sometimes her dog Casper sat at the window and caught flies. But then she had wanted everyone to laugh.

This was different.

At recess Leonard and Douglas Cunningham and Thomas Messer waved twigs at her.

"Here, giraff-ie!" Leonard said in a high voice. "Come here, girl. Come on!"

He said it the way Daphne sometimes called Casper to come in for the night.

"Shut up," she said.

"You look just like a giraffe. Even your freckles," Douglas yelled. "Like a giraffe's spots!"

"Get out of here!" Louisa yelled back. "Or we're going to kiss you!"

"I don't want to be kissed by an old giraffe!" Leonard said. He and the other boys ran off screaming.

"They are so rotten," Daphne said to Louisa.

"They're just boys," Louisa said, flicking her hair over her shoulder the way she always did. Usually it got on Daphne's nerves. But not today.

Today, for the first time in her life, she was wishing she weren't so tall.

.....

"Daphne El, just look at those jeans!"

"What?"

Grandma sat back on her heels. She squinted up from under the brow of her big, floppy straw hat. "I swear, they barely cover your knees!" she said.

Daphne looked down. "You can't see my knees, Grandma," she said. But her ankles were plain as day.

Grandma clicked her tongue against her teeth. "I say it's time for some shopping."

"These jeans are fine," Daphne said. "Just about soft enough."

She kneeled down to help Grandma. As she did, the buttons at her waist snapped open.

Grandma rested her gloved hands on her thighs. "Time for new clothes, Daphne El," she said. "You're growing like a weed."

"A weed," Daphne said. Something too tall. Something no one wanted. "Great."

"It's just an expression," Grandma said, leaning forward to pick up her trowel. "Hand me those delphiniums, Daphne El."

Grandma loved to work in Daphne's garden, since she lived in an apartment and only had room on her balcony for pots of geraniums.

Daphne handed Grandma the flat of seedlings.

"Grandma?" Daphne asked. "How come I'm so tall?"

Grandma wiped sweat off her forehead with her arm. "Because I'm tall, I guess," she said. "Five eight is tall for a woman my age. And your mom's tall, too." She worked the soil with her trowel. "And your dad was a tall man. Well over six feet. So it's right for you to be tall."

Daphne's dad had died when she was a baby. Usually she loved being like him.

"I wish my dad had been short," Daphne said.

"How come?" Grandma asked.

"Because if he were short, and Mom is tall, then I would be somewhere in the middle," Daphne said.

Grandma eased a seedling out of its plastic pot and set it gently in the hole she had dug. "It might not have worked out that way," she said. "Besides, your dad's being tall was part of him. He stood up for people who got picked on. He nursed sick animals back to health. He was tall. All those things together." She patted wet soil around her delphinium. "If he hadn't been tall, he would have been a different man."

"If I weren't tall, I'd still be me," Daphne said. "Only short."

"It doesn't work like that, Daphne El," Grandma said.

11

Chapter 2

One day, during math, Mrs. Jefferson asked, "Who wants to volunteer?"

Daphne raised her hand. She loved math.

"All right, Daphne," Mrs. Jefferson said. "Your age times four equals what?"

"Cinchy," Daphne said. She bit her lower lip and sat on her hands, so Mrs. Jefferson would see that she didn't need to count her fingers. "Thirty-two," she said.

"Very good," Mrs. Jefferson said. She looked out over the class. "How old is Daphne?" she asked.

Leonard DiMaggio raised his hand. "At least ten," he said. "My mom says Daphne must have been held back and that's why she's so tall."

"I AM EIGHT YEARS OLD," Daphne yelled before Mrs. Jefferson could say anything. "For your information!"

Kids didn't yell in class every day. It was very exciting. Everyone started talking and laughing at once.

"Quiet, class!" Mrs. Jefferson said, clapping her hands.

Daphne's face felt hot.

When the class was quiet, Mrs. Jefferson looked at Daphne.

"Of course you're eight, Daphne," she said sweetly. "We all know that." She turned to look just at Leonard. "Don't we, Leonard?"

Leonard nodded yes. But when Mrs. Jefferson turned back to the chalkboard, he looked at Daphne and stuck out his tongue and then made his mouth say "Ten" without any sound coming out.

At recess Daphne headed for the swings. Louisa caught up.

"I told Leonard I was at your eighth birthday party," she said. "I told him your mom lit eight candles and everything."

"Thanks," Daphne said.

"Let's play hairdresser," Louisa said. "You can braid my hair, if you want."

She was trying to be nice.

"I don't think I feel like playing hairdresser right now," Daphne said.

She didn't feel like doing anything. Nothing seemed like any fun as long as Leonard DiMaggio's mother was going around telling people that she'd been held back.

She sat on the swings for the whole recess, wondering how you got a grownup to stop telling lies about you. And wishing her father had been short.

·····

"Tomorrow we start our new science unit," Mrs. Jefferson told the class. "Blood and Guts."

Some of the boys hooted and pretended to shoot each other and die.

"We will be dissecting lambs' eyes," Mrs. Jefferson said. *"Dissecting* means 'taking apart.' Scientists dissect animals' body parts to find out how they work. It's a way of learning more about how human bodies work, and how to keep them healthy."

Daphne wrote *Cool!* on the cover of her notebook and turned it so Louisa could see. Louisa leaned over to read what Daphne had written. Then she looked up at Daphne and smiled.

"Everyone," Mrs. Jefferson said, "will need a partner."

Uh-oh, Daphne thought. Mrs. Jefferson assigned partners. She didn't let the kids pick their own partners because she said they always picked their friends and never got a chance to work with someone new.

Mrs. Jefferson started reading down her list. Daphne crossed all her fingers and hoped she got Louisa.

"Leonard DiMaggio," Mrs. Jefferson said, "and Daphne Slater."

"Rats!" Daphne said. She couldn't help it.

"Daphne, how would you like to eat lunch at your desk for a week?" Mrs. Jefferson asked. Daphne knew that she had rules about hurting people's feelings.

"Sorry," she said. Even though Mrs. Jefferson doesn't know about people like Leonard DiMaggio, she thought. Whose feelings you're not supposed to hurt even though he does things like make you hate third grade.

Leonard didn't say anything. He didn't gag and grab his throat when Mrs. Jefferson explained how they were going to slice open the sclera. He didn't lick his lips and say "Ah-h-h!" when she told everyone how the vitreous humor would feel a lot like Jell-O. Daphne kept thinking he would yell out, "At least it's not a giraffe eyeball!" and fall over laughing. But he didn't.

He just sat there.

.....

Every Tuesday Grandma came over for dinner and to play cards. Mom always tried to cook something new on Tuesdays. Tonight it was pasta with four cheeses.

Daphne finished her pasta.

"May I be excused, please?" she asked.

"Sure," Mom said.

"The deck's in the bottom drawer," Grandma said.

"I don't feel like playing cards, Grandma," Daphne said.

"Are you all right?" Mom asked.

"Yeah," Daphne said. "I've just got stuff I have to do."

Casper followed her down the hall, his toenails clicking on the floor. Daphne flicked on the light in the back bedroom. There was an old green file cabinet in the closet where Mom kept things like important papers and extra house keys.

Daphne pulled open the heavy metal drawer and started flipping through files until she came to the one marked *Daphne Eloise.* She sat down on the floor. Casper circled three times and sat down next to her, shoving his back end up against her leg.

There were all kinds of cool things in that file. Some of Daphne's baby hair. Cards from her aunts and uncles congratulating her for being born. A Social Security card, whatever that was. Her first and second grade report cards.

Daphne had so much fun looking at everything that she almost forgot what she was trying to find. Until she found it.

Her birth certificate. She remembered waiting in a long line with Mom to get it. Mom had explained, "This piece of paper tells all kinds of things about the day you were born."

She read her name and the name of the hospital where she was born and the name of the doctor. She read her mom's name. And her dad's, Roger Slater. Her eyes always stung a little when she saw his name. Seeing his name reminded her that he was a real person. Someone she missed.

She finally found it. *Date of birth.*

She figured it out.

She was eight. Just as Mom said. Just as she thought.

She put everything away. Drat that old Mrs. DiMaggio, she thought, closing the file cabinet drawer.

She was very relieved.

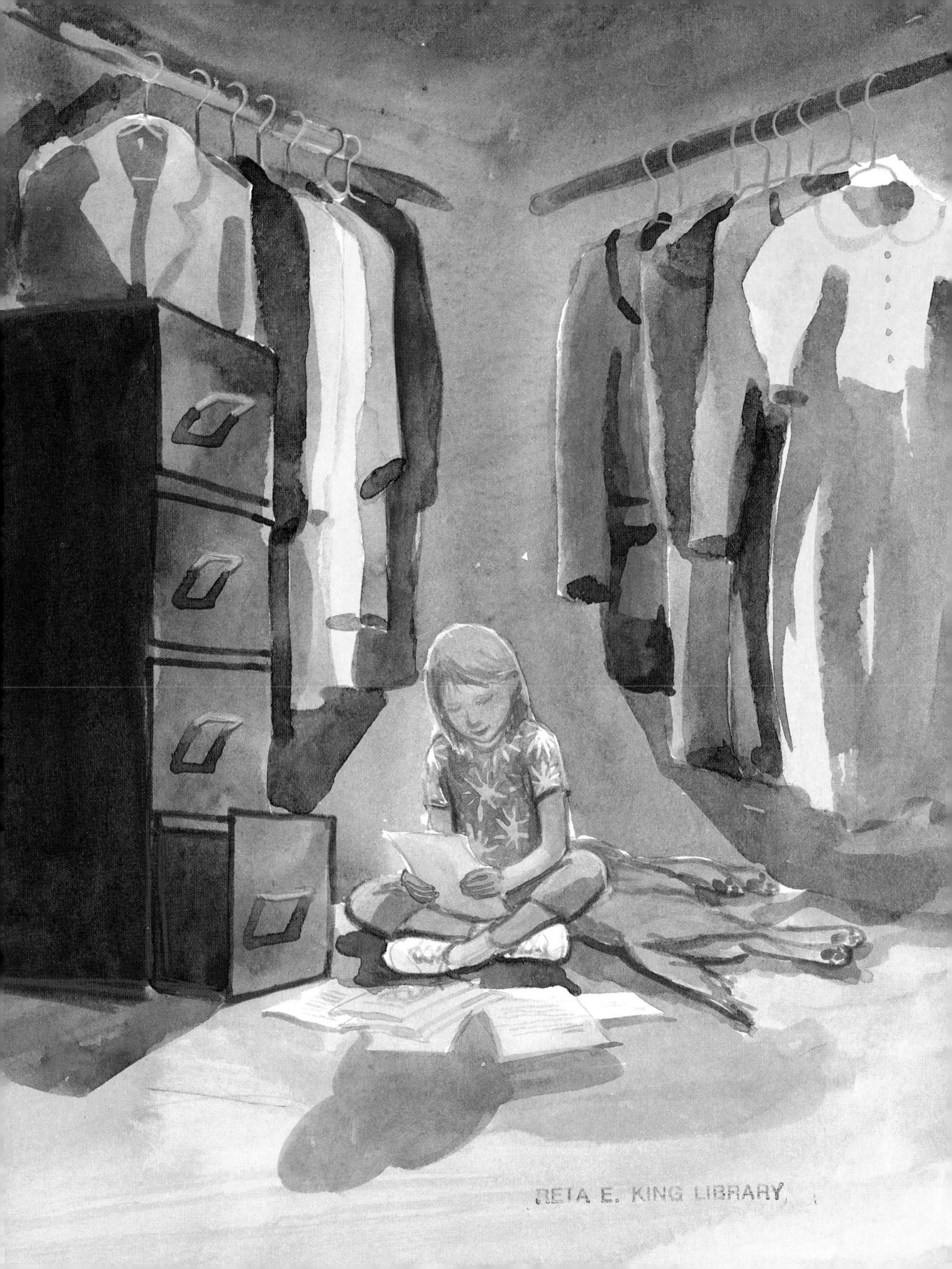

Chapter 3

The next day, after lunch, Mrs. Jefferson made all the kids change seats so that they could sit next to their partners.

Daphne had figured out just what to say.

"Listen, Leonard," she said. She tried to talk loudly enough to sound like she meant business, but not so loudly that everyone else would hear. "You better not get any eyeball on me or I'm telling."

Leonard was scribbling on a piece of paper. He didn't even look up.

"I mean it, Leonard," she said. She just had a feeling about Leonard. That he was the kind of kid who would stick a lamb eyeball in your lunch box and think it was funny.

"Shut up," Leonard said, but not like he meant it.

"Quiet, class!" Mrs. Jefferson said. She waited a few seconds and then looked sternly at Jessica Peterson and Frances McHale. "Whispering is still talking, ladies."

The kids wanted to get the eyeballs, but Mrs. Jefferson made them learn things about eyes first. She gave them pieces of paper, each with a picture of an eye on it. They had to label all the parts.

She showed them where the tear ducts were, and the cornea, and the iris.

"See the dark spot?" she asked. "It's really a hole that lets the light through. It's called the pupil."

"You mean there's a hole in your eye?" a boy called out.

"Raise your hand, Kenny," Mrs. Jefferson said.

Daphne raised her hand.

"How come you can't just take a needle and poke it in there?" she asked.

Everyone groaned.

"That's a good question, Daphne," Mrs. Jefferson said. "It's because the cornea covers the hole, and it's tough. Very tough."

Just at that moment, Leonard sighed. A loud sigh. But then he said something very softly—whispered it, almost—so that no one but Daphne could hear. "I just can't do this."

Mrs. Jefferson was starting to explain about aqueous fluid.

"What?" Daphne whispered back. "Listen, Leonard. You can't make me do everything. Or I'll tell."

Leonard shook his head. "I mean I really *can't*," he said.

"Why not?"

"Because," he whispered back, *"it's a lamb's eye!"*

He looked terrified.

"So?" Daphne said.

"I mean, a real lamb!" he hissed back. "With curly fur and a wet, black nose. Like at my grandpa's farm." He looked miserable. "I just can't," he said.

"Leonard and Daphne," Mrs. Jefferson said, "would you like to share your insights with the class?"

Daphne knew that was Mrs. Jefferson's fancy way of telling them to shut up.

"Now," Mrs. Jefferson said when they were quiet, "we're going to do an experiment. Everyone close one eye."

Everyone did.

"Hold your hands out like this," Mrs. Jefferson said. "Point your index fingers. Now bring your hands together and try to touch your index fingers to each other, keeping one eye closed."

It was hard. Daphne's index fingers wouldn't touch.

"Everything looks flat if you're using only one eye," Mrs. Jefferson said. "With two eyes, we have depth perception. Things look the way they really are."

The room was getting noisy again. All the boys were pretending to be drunk. So no one else heard when Leonard said, "Doesn't it bother you?"

"What?"

"That it's a real lamb's eye. From a real lamb."

"No," Daphne said. Even though she hadn't really thought about it before. "I mean, I eat lamb chops and I don't think about them being from real lambs."

"But they *are*," Leonard said quietly.

It was hard to believe that this was the same kid who was always making fun of Daphne and calling her names.

"Are you faking?" Daphne asked.

Leonard shook his head. "I'm not faking," he said.

Mrs. Jefferson was passing out scalpels. "You'll want to slice through the cornea and into the sclera. Then you'll see the vitreous humor oozing out," she said. "Be careful! Scalpels are sharp!"

Daphne had seen Leonard hold a sea cucumber on a field trip to the aquarium in second grade. The sea cucumber was fat and slimy, but Leonard hadn't minded at all. Now, just hearing about vitreous humor, he looked like he was going to throw up.

The kids started cutting into their eyeballs.

"What about scientists learning about how things work?" Daphne asked Leonard. "What about keeping human bodies healthy?"

"I know," he said. "My dad says they couldn't make medicine if they didn't take animals apart to find out how they work." He chewed on his pencil eraser. "I just wish it didn't have to be *lambs*," he said. "Sharks, maybe. Or crocodiles."

Talking about lambs, Leonard sounded as if he really loved them. Maybe he wasn't all bad, Daphne thought. Someone who loved lambs couldn't be all bad.

"I'll do the cutting," she said. "You can pretend to be writing stuff down."

Leonard didn't say anything, but he looked relieved.

Cutting wasn't so bad. It was a little like cutting into a cherry tomato. Squishy.

Daphne looked for the optic nerve while Mrs. Jefferson explained about rods and cones. "They help you see color, and black and white," she said. "Many animals do not see in color."

Daphne tried to imagine what that would be like. The world would look gray and shadowy. Everything would look like everything else. Even with two eyes, it would be hard to tell how things really were.

Mrs. Jefferson leaned over Daphne's shoulder. "That really bright blue stuff is called tapetum," she said, pointing. "It helps animals see well at night."

When she walked away, Daphne said, "Don't you want to look, Leonard? It's pretty. Really."

Leonard, who had been pretending to look for something in his desk when Mrs. Jefferson was leaning over Daphne, said, "No."

It was almost time to stop. Most of the eyeballs looked like big gloppy messes by now. Tony Blankenship was yelling "Yee-haw!" and waving his optic nerve over his head like a lasso. All the kids were laughing. Except Leonard and Daphne.

Daphne was thinking, That optic nerve used to belong to a lamb. With curly fur and a wet, black nose.

It didn't seem right, waving it around like that.

Mrs. Jefferson was passing out pieces of newspaper. "Wrap your eyeballs in these and throw them away," she said. "Then go to the sink and wash your hands."

Everyone stood in line waiting for a turn at the sink. Leonard washed his hands even though he hadn't gotten any eyeball on them. Daphne waited behind him.

While he dried his hands, Daphne was soaping hers.

"So," he finally said. "Are you going to tell?"

"Tell what?"

"About me liking lambs and everything."

Daphne thought about it.

"No," she said. "I won't tell."

He didn't even say thanks.

Chapter 4

The next day, at snack recess, Leonard and Douglas and Thomas started waving twigs at Daphne.

"Nice green leaves, giraff-ie," Leonard said. "Come get a nice snack, girl."

Daphne couldn't believe it.

After she'd said she wouldn't tell.

"Don't pay any attention," Louisa said. She offered Daphne some of her vanilla pudding cup.

Daphne almost told her. She would have made it really good, too. How Leonard was making little urpy sounds in his throat. How he begged her not to tell anyone.

But she didn't.

She'd said she wouldn't, and so she didn't.

She always kept her promises. It's just something about me, she thought. Like liking science. And being tall.

All those things together.

Daphne and Louisa finished the pudding cup. Daphne thought, I'm actually a pretty nice kid.

· · · · ·

"Daphne El, what are you doing?" Grandma asked. Mom stood behind her, blowing on her coffee and looking at Daphne over Grandma's shoulder.

Daphne was sitting on the kitchen floor. Casper was sitting in front of her. She was holding his big, furry head in her hand and looking into his eyes. Casper had that funny look on his face, the one Grandma called his trying-to-look-intelligent look.

"Trying to figure out what he sees," Daphne said. "What he really sees."

"Food. Chew toys. Other dogs," Grandma said. "You."

"Mrs. Jefferson says animals see in black and white," Daphne said.

"I guess I knew that," Mom said.

Daphne thought about how Casper lay on her feet when she was sick. He didn't even have to hear her voice. He just knew.

Or how he knew when she was going to take him for a walk. If she got up from the couch to get an apple or walked into the room looking for her lunch box, he looked up and wagged his tail. But if Daphne got up from the couch or walked into the room thinking, *I'm going to walk Casper,* he jumped on her and yipped and followed her to the door.

Somehow Casper just knew.

"But he sees things. Things even I don't see," she said. "Even though everything looks black and white to him. He knows things."

"Animals are like that," Grandma said, scooching down and scratching Casper's head.

Daphne looked deep into Casper's eyes. "How does he do that?" she asked.

"It's a mystery," Mom said.

Casper wagged his tail. Daphne could tell he was trying to look really intelligent.

The rest of Blood and Guts was fun. The kids built a skeleton out of tongue depressors. On the last day they scraped the insides of their cheeks with toothpicks and looked at them under microscopes. There was gross stuff on those toothpicks.

Daphne hung around until Leonard had finished looking at his toothpick under the microscope.

"What?" Leonard asked impatiently.

"It's just—" Daphne stopped and started over. "It's just that if I ever have to dissect any parts again, I think I'm going to ask if I can go to the library or clean out my desk instead." She paused. "For your information."

She'd been thinking about the animals those parts came from. She couldn't help it. Maybe those animals understood things. Maybe they had a trying-to-look-intelligent look.

She would never have thought about those animals if it hadn't been for Leonard.

Leonard didn't say anything for a while. Then he looked out the window, as if he were pretending that he wasn't really talking. "In fourth grade you don't do Blood and Guts," he said. "You do Volcanoes and Seeds." He stopped and looked at Daphne. "But I guess that's good. What you said."

It's weird about Leonard, Daphne thought. He steps on the sand mountains the first graders build. He makes fun of the slow reading group.

And he loves lambs.

It's just like Grandma said, she thought.

He's all those things together.

Leonard was starting to look uncomfortable. As if he'd been nice for too long.

"You still look like a giraffe, you know," he said. "You're still tall enough to be ten."

"I'm tall for my age," Daphne said proudly. "Like my dad."

Leonard shrugged.

"And you're still the rottenest kid in third grade," she said.

That was all she had meant to say, but at the last minute, she changed her mind.

"Most of the time," she added.